THE FRIENDLY FOAL

Suddenly, Mandy heard a noise. It sounded like little hooves . . .

She turned round. "Look, it's Fern!" she cried. "I see what you mean. She's a *very* friendly foal!"

When you've enjoyed all the
Little Animal Ark books
you might enjoy two other series
about Mandy Hope, also by Lucy Daniels –
Animal Ark Pets and Animal Ark

LUCY DANIELS

The Friendly Foal

Illustrated by Georgie Ripper

Hodder
Children's
Books

a division of Hodder Headline Limited

Special thanks to Gill Harvey

Little Animal Ark is a trademark of Working Partners Limited
Text copyright © 2003 Working Partners Limited
Created by Working Partners Limited, London, W6 0QT
Illustrations copyright © 2003 Georgie Ripper
Cover illustration copyright © 2003 Andy Ellis

First published in Great Britain in 2003
by Hodder Children's Books

4

A Catalogue record for this book is available from the
British Library

ISBN-10: 0 340 87386 8
ISBN-13: 978 0 340 87386 8

Printed and bound in Great Britain by
Clays Ltd, St Ives Plc, Bungay, Suffolk

The paper and board used in this paperback by Hodder Children's
Books are natural recyclable products made from wood grown in
sustainable forests. The manufacturing processes conform to the
environmental regulations of the country of origin.

Hodder Children's Books
A division of Hodder Headline Limited
338 Euston Road, London NW1 3BH

Chapter One

"Mum! Look! There's Helen!" said Mandy Hope, pointing out of the Land-rover window.

Helen Cook, one of Mandy's friends from school, was jumping up and down outside the old stone farmhouse where she lived. She had a *huge* smile on her face.

"She looks even more excited than you," laughed Mrs Hope, as she parked the Land-rover.

Helen's pony, Bluebell, had given birth to a foal just three days ago. Mrs Hope had come to check mother and baby over. Both Mandy's parents were vets, which was great for Mandy because she was mad about animals! Sometimes she got to go on her mum's visits, especially in the summer holidays. Today, Helen had invited Mandy to stay at Willow Farm all day.

Mandy undid her seat belt and clambered out of the car as fast as she could.

"Mandy!" Helen burst out, running up to her. "You are going to *love* Fern. She is the sweetest foal in the whole world!"

Mandy and Helen ran inside to say hello to Mrs Cook, while Mandy's mum got her vet's bag out of the car.

"Lemon squash, Mandy?" smiled Mrs Cook.

"Oh yes, please," said Mandy. "Where's Fern?"

"She's in a pen with Bluebell," said Helen, as Mrs Hope came in with her bag. "Dad made it specially. Bluebell's stable isn't really big enough for the two of them. Fern likes to run around already!"

"But she's only three days old!" Mandy gasped.

"In the wild, foals need to run when they're a few *hours* old," said Mrs Hope. "If they couldn't, other animals like wolves would gobble them up!"

"Well, Fern would *definitely* be able to run away," said Helen proudly. "By the time we move to Dorset, she'll be able to run faster than me!"

"I expect she can already," Mrs Hope said with a smile.

The Cooks were moving to Dorset soon. Mandy was sad that they were going, but there was still time for her to get to know Fern before they went. She couldn't wait to see her! She drank her squash in one big gulp. Then she and her mum followed Helen and Mrs Cook out to the barn.

As Mrs Cook opened the barn

door, Mandy peered inside. Bluebell stood knee-deep in straw, munching a mouthful of hay. And there beside her was Fern.

"Oh!" said Mandy in surprise. "She's black and white!"

"Yes," said Helen. "She looks like her dad. Isn't she *lovely*?"

Mandy had expected the foal to look like Bluebell. Helen's pony was a pretty grey colour, which Helen said was called blue roan. But Fern was white with big black patches. Her mane and tail were black and fluffy.

"She's *wonderful*!" Mandy breathed. "She looks just like a circus pony!"

Helen laughed, and carefully opened the gate of the pen to let everyone in.

Fern trotted over straight away. "She's really friendly," said Helen, reaching out to stroke Fern's neck.

"Yes. A bit *too* friendly!" said Mrs Cook.

"How can she be too friendly?" Mandy asked, puzzled.

"Fern loves being with people," Helen explained. "She doesn't understand why she can't be with us *all* the time!"

"Well, she looks very strong and healthy," said Mrs Hope. She knelt beside Fern and looked in her eyes and mouth. Then she ran a hand over her tummy.

"I'll just check her mum," said Mrs Hope, when she'd finished.

Fern nuzzled Helen's coat.

"Can I pat her?" Mandy asked Helen.

"Oh yes, she loves it!" said Helen.

So Mandy patted Fern's neck, then stroked her little tufty mane.

"She likes it when you scratch her neck, near her ears," said Helen.

Fern was so small that her ears were easy to reach. Mandy rubbed just behind them. The foal's coat was lovely and soft, like velvet. Fern gave a little snort. She was enjoying all the fuss!

"Well, everything's fine," said Mandy's mum, patting Bluebell's neck. "I'd better be going now. I've got three more visits to do today."

"Let's go and say goodbye to your mum, then we can come back and play with Fern," said Helen. They left Fern and Bluebell in their pen, and walked with Mrs Hope towards the house.

Suddenly, Mandy heard a noise. It sounded like little hooves . . .

She turned round. "Look, it's Fern!" she cried.

"Fern!" exclaimed Mrs Cook. "How did you get out?"

Fern gave a little whinny and trotted straight up to Helen.

"She must have squeezed through a gap in the pen to follow us," said Helen.

"I see what you mean," Mandy laughed. "She's a *very* friendly foal!"

Chapter Two

Mrs Hope waved goodbye and climbed into the Land-rover. When she had gone, Helen and Mandy led Fern back to her pen, each holding a tuft of her fluffy mane.

Fern trotted straight over to Bluebell. She ducked under her mother's tummy and began to suckle, her stubby tail waggling to and fro.

Mandy smiled. "She looks really hungry," she said. "It must be her lunch time."

Helen nodded. "I wonder how she got out?" she said.

They both looked round the pen.

"Look, there's a little gap here, between the rails and the gate," said Mandy. "Maybe we could block it up with some straw."

"That's a good idea," agreed Helen.

They stuffed the gap with handfuls of thick yellow straw. Then they let themselves out of the pen.

"Let's go now, before Fern finishes drinking," whispered Helen. "Or she might try to follow us again!"

They tiptoed out of the barn, hoping that the foal wouldn't notice.

"You're just in time for lunch, you two!" said Mrs Cook,

as they walked into the farmhouse. She put a plate of sandwiches on the table.

They were just about to sit down when a little nose poked round the kitchen door. The door opened wider . . . and wider. With a patter of soft hooves, Fern pushed right into the kitchen.

"Fern!" gasped Helen. "You've found us again!"

Mandy thought Fern looked very sweet, peering around.

But Mrs Cook wasn't so pleased. "Look at my clean floor," she said crossly. "It's covered in hoofprints. And I'd only just mopped it!"

Helen and Mandy looked at each other. It was hard not to laugh – especially when Fern walked over to the bucket in the corner and nibbled the mop!

"Well! That foal's got some cheek," said Mrs Cook. But Mandy was glad to see that she was smiling.

"What's going on?" said a voice. It was Mr Cook, Helen's dad. He was standing in the doorway, looking amazed.

"Fern wants to live in the

house with us," said Helen.

"I'm afraid she'll have to learn that everyone has a home," said Mrs Cook firmly. "And hers is *not* in the kitchen!"

Mr Cook sat down at the table with Helen and Mandy. "How did Fern get out?" he asked.

"There's a gap in her pen," explained Helen. "We blocked it up with straw, but she still escaped!"

"I think I'd better take a look at it after lunch," said Mr Cook.

Helen and Mandy ate their sandwiches. Then they went back to the barn with Mr Cook, taking Fern with them.

Bluebell was dozing in the pen, resting one hind leg. Fern went over to her mum while Mr Cook looked at the gap in the fence.

"Will you be able to fix it?" Mandy asked. Helen's dad was a carpenter, and he had a big van full of tools and pieces of wood.

Mr Cook nodded. "Oh yes, I've got just the right sized plank in my van," he said. "But first, here's a present for Fern."

"A present?" echoed Helen. She looked excitedly at Mandy.

Mr Cook took a brown paper bag out of his pocket. He gave it to Helen, who looked inside.

"What is it?" asked Mandy.

A big smile spread across Helen's face as she pulled out a tiny lilac headcollar. "Look! It's perfect for Fern!" she exclaimed.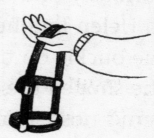

"You can try it out while I fetch the plank from my van," said Mr Cook. "Put it on slowly, though. Fern might not like it at first." He opened the gate and went out of the barn.

Helen called Fern over and showed her the headcollar. "Look, this is for you!" she said.

"It's what grown-up horses wear," Mandy told the foal.

Fern sniffed the headcollar curiously and tried to nibble it. Helen laughed and undid the buckle on the side. Then she slipped the headcollar over Fern's nose. Mandy stroked the foal's neck as Helen fitted the

strap behind Fern's ears and
fastened the buckle.

Fern shook her head, but
the headcollar didn't come off.
Then she bent down and tried
to paw at it with her front hoof.
Helen and Mandy patted her,
to reassure her.

"It must feel really strange," Mandy said.

Just then, Mr Cook came back with a piece of wood and his tools. Fern forgot about the headcollar at once. She let out a tiny whinny and trotted over to see what he was doing.

Mr Cook nailed the piece of wood across the gap.

"There," he said, as Fern sniffed at the plank. "That should keep you in, all right. You can

take Fern's headcollar off now, Helen. We can put it on again tomorrow."

Helen and Mandy took off Fern's new headcollar, then let themselves out of the pen. They looked over the gate. Fern was still nosing the new piece of wood, looking puzzled.

"Sorry, Fern," said Helen. "You won't be able to follow us indoors any more!"

Chapter Three

"I hear you're off to the Cooks' again today," said Mandy's dad, helping himself to more potatoes.

"Yes," Mandy said. "It's only a week until they move to Dorset. So I want to see Helen and Fern as much as I can before they go!"

The Hopes were having lunch. It was Mandy's favourite – fish fingers, boiled potatoes and peas. But she was almost too excited to eat, because she was going to see Fern again! As she swallowed her last mouthful, she heard a car drawing up outside. She looked out of the window.

"It's Mrs Cook and Helen!" said Mandy. "May I leave the table?"

"Of course," said Mrs Hope. "Off you go. Have a nice time, love."

Mandy rushed out to the car. "How's Fern?" she asked as she clambered in.

"She's fine," said Helen. "Mum says we can lead her around outside today. She really likes her headcollar now."

Mandy beamed at her friend.

When they arrived at the farmhouse, Mrs Cook gave them a purple lead rope to clip on to Fern's headcollar. Then Mandy and Helen went to the barn.

Fern looked very happy to see them.

"She's grown!" Mandy said. "In just three days!"

"Yes," said Helen. "She's much stronger, too."

She opened the gate and clipped the lead rope to Fern's headcollar. "Come on, girl!" she said, clicking her tongue. "You can come out to play!"

At first, Fern didn't understand how to follow the lead rope. When she felt it tug against her head, she stopped, looking puzzled.

Then she walked forward in a rush, and bumped into Mandy.

"Steady, Fern!" laughed Helen.

Slowly, they made their way out of the barn, taking turns to lead her. Mandy knew she had to stay level with Fern's shoulder while she walked, not just pull her along. It wasn't easy. Fern wanted to stop and look at everything!

"I don't think she knows that *we're* meant to be leading *her*," Mandy joked.

But soon, Fern began to get the hang of it. They led her out past the stable block to the big garden in front of the farmhouse.

"I know what," said Helen. "Let's play hide and seek. You go and hide with Fern, then I'll come and look for you both."

Mandy grinned. What a great idea! She took Fern's lead rope. "Count to fifty," she called, as Helen covered her eyes.

"Where shall we go, Fern?" Mandy whispered. She looked round. There were some big bushes at the end of the garden. They would be perfect to hide behind! Quickly, she gave Fern's lead rope a little tug, and Fern trotted after her.

Mandy crouched down next to the foal behind the bushes. "She won't find us here," she whispered, patting Fern's neck. "But you mustn't make any noise!"

Fern shook her head with a little snort.

"Shhh!" Mandy laughed. Then she listened carefully.

"Forty-eight, forty-nine, FIFTY!" Helen shouted. "Coming!"

Mandy stayed very still. How long would it take Helen to find them?

To her surprise, Helen appeared around the bushes at once. "Found you!" she cried.

"That was quick!" Mandy
said. "How did you know where
to look?"

Helen pointed to the grass.
There were little hoofprints
leading straight across the lawn!

"Oh dear," said Mandy, laughing. "Fern makes this game too easy."

"And she's covered in bits of leaf now," said Helen. "Let's take her back to the barn and brush them off."

Helen fetched a soft body brush from the tack room. She showed Mandy how to brush Fern in the same direction that her hair grew – down her neck, along her back, then down her legs, too.

"My mum says it's good for her to be brushed," said Helen. "It keeps her coat clean and helps her feel safe around us."

Mandy stopped for a moment and smiled. The little foal was arching her neck prettily with her ears pricked forward.

"I think she likes being brushed!" she said.

They laughed as Fern turned and nudged the brush in Mandy's hand.

Suddenly, Helen looked sad. "Fern loves people so much," she said. "She's going to miss having my friends to play with. What if she's really lonely when we move to Dorset?"

Chapter Four

Mandy was surprised. She hadn't thought of that. "Don't worry, Helen," she said. "You'll make lots of new friends in Dorset! Especially when they hear you have a lovely foal to play with."

Helen put her arms around Fern's neck. "Maybe," she said. "But school won't start for weeks after we move. Fern will really miss everyone here."

Mandy brushed a leaf out of the foal's tufty tail, thinking hard. "She'll still have you," she said. "You're the person she loves most of all."

The foal whickered softly. Helen smiled, and kissed her nose. "That's true," she agreed.

But Mandy could see that Helen was still worried.

Just then, Mandy heard the sound of her mum's Land-rover in the driveway. She went to say goodbye to Mrs Cook, then climbed into the car next to her mum.

"Bye, Helen," she called out of the window. "Thank you for a lovely day!"

Mrs Hope was just about to drive away when Helen gasped and put her hand over her mouth.

"Wait!" she shouted, and ran into the farmhouse. In a few moments she ran back out again and handed Mandy a rainbow-coloured envelope.

There was a sparkly pink invitation inside.

"I'm having a goodbye party for all my friends," Helen explained. "It's this Saturday.

I hope you can come!"

"Oh! I can go, can't I, Mum?" Mandy asked.

"Of course you can," smiled Mrs Hope. "I know you wouldn't want to miss a treat like that!"

Saturday arrived at last. Mandy put on her best blue T-shirt and her bright yellow trousers. She wrapped Helen's present, a pretty pink photo frame, and wrote in her card.

Goodbye, Helen and Fern, she wrote. *I hope you make lots of new friends in Dorset. Love from Mandy.*

"I wish Helen wasn't moving," she said with a sigh, as her mum drove her over to Willow Farm.

"But you can still write to her," said Mrs Hope.

Mandy smiled. "I suppose so," she agreed. "Helen might even send me some photos of Fern!"

There were lots of cars in the driveway to Willow Farm. "Look, there's Ben!" Mandy said, pointing to her friend Ben Stokes.

She jumped out of the car, eager
to see who else had arrived.

"Bye, love," called Mrs Hope.
"Have a nice time!"

In the kitchen, Mrs Cook
was handing out paper cups of
orange squash. All Mandy's
school friends were there –
Richard Tanner, and Jill Redfern,
and Laura and Sally. It was a bit
like being back at school again,
only much more fun.

"Mandy!" cried Helen,
running to give her friend a hug.

Mandy gave Helen her
present. Helen's face broke into
a big smile when she saw what
it was.

"I'll put a picture of Fern in it!" she said.

Just then, Mr Cook clapped his hands. "Is everyone here?" he called.

Helen looked round and nodded.

"Let's go outside for the surprise, then," said Mr Cook mysteriously. "Come on, everyone!"

Mandy's heart thumped with excitement. A surprise? She looked at Helen, but Helen just grinned back, her eyes sparkling. Mr Cook led them through the garden, past the

stable block, past the barn . . .
Where were they going? Mandy
wondered.

At last, they reached the
paddock. And there was Mandy's
friend Pippa Simkins. Mandy
looked behind Pippa – and saw
her dad, with Sparky, the Party
Pony!

"Hurray!" cheered everyone.
"Pony rides!"

Mandy jumped up and down
in delight. She'd ridden Sparky
before, at Sarah Drummond's
party. She couldn't wait to ride
him again!

"Now," said Mr Simkins.
"Who wants the first ride?"

Jill Redfern stuck her hand in the air. "Me, please!" she said.

Mr Simkins gave her a hard hat to wear. Then he lifted her on to Sparky's back, and they set off round the paddock.

"Isn't it a great surprise? We couldn't use Bluebell," Helen explained to Mandy.

"It's too soon to ride her, after giving birth to Fern."

"Never mind. Sparky's lovely!" said Mandy, watching the pony break into a trot.

"Oh yes," said Helen. "Sparky's a brilliant Party Pony. I'm really lucky to have him here for the day!"

Chapter Five

Riding Sparky was just as wonderful as Mandy remembered. She loved it when he trotted, and she had to rise up and down in time with his bouncy strides. She wished she could ride him for ever! But soon it was someone else's turn.

She didn't mind, because after the pony rides, Helen took them to the barn to see Fern.

She looked really pleased to see everyone! She pressed up against the side of the pen, making little whickering noises.

"She wants to come and play with us!" Mandy laughed.

"I'll ask my mum if she can," said Helen. "Sparky won't mind, will he, Pippa?"

"No, he loves meeting other horses," said Pippa.

Helen and Mandy went up to the house and asked Mrs Cook if they could let Fern out.

"Of course," said Mrs Cook.

Helen took Fern's lilac head-collar and they went back to the barn.

"You can lead her, Mandy," Helen said kindly. "She knows you almost as well as she knows me!"

Mandy beamed as she led the foal into the garden. Fern danced at the end of the lead rope. She seemed really excited to see so many new faces!

Ben Stokes came over to pat her, and she tried to nibble his tufty hair.

"Your hair must look like tasty hay!" Mandy teased him.

Then Pippa brought Sparky over to meet the foal. Sparky pricked his ears forward – and so did Fern. They touched noses and blew warm breath at each other.

"Fern's so friendly," laughed Mandy. "She likes other horses, too, not just people!"

Just then, Mrs Cook called everyone over to the big garden table for tea. There were sandwiches and slices of pizza, then cake and ice cream. Mr Simkins and Ben's dad, Mr Stokes, held Fern and Sparky while everyone ate. Fern looked tiny, standing next to Sparky!

When no one could eat any more, Mr Cook clapped

his hands. "How about a sack race?" he said.

"Yes, please!" everyone shouted.

So Mr Cook fetched lots of big plastic feed sacks from the barn, and lined everyone up.

"We can't leave Fern out," said Mandy.

"No," agreed Helen. "I'll lead her!"

But Fern didn't understand sack races. She was so excited when everyone began to hop that she trotted forward at top speed, dragging Helen after her. Helen lost her balance and fell over!

Mandy laughed so much that she couldn't hop properly. Richard Tanner won the race by miles!

They were all having such fun that they couldn't believe it when Mrs Tanner arrived to collect

Richard, then Mr Redfern came for Jill. Soon Laura and Sally had to go, too. Then Ben. Only Pippa, Mandy and Helen were left.

They sat on the lawn. Pippa was holding Sparky's lead rope, and Mandy was holding Fern's. Fern kept trying to nibble Sparky's tail, and Mandy had to pull him away.

But Sparky was very patient. He didn't mind a bit.

It had been such a lovely day, and Fern had made so many new friends! It was a shame that she wouldn't have the chance to meet them all again. Mandy looked at Helen, and saw that she

was looking a little bit sad. She'd
soon be leaving all her friends
behind, too . . .

Suddenly, Mandy had an idea.
"Helen," she said. "Why don't
you make Fern a Party Pony when
you go to Dorset? Your dad could
tell all his new customers about
her!"

Helen's face lit up for a
moment. Then she frowned. "But

she's too young," she said. "She couldn't give any rides."

"That doesn't matter," said Pippa. "She's so sweet that everyone will love playing with her!"

Helen grinned. "That's true," she said. "Then I'd make lots of new friends, and Fern would never be lonely."

"No," said Mandy. "She can be as friendly as she likes!"

Do you love animals? So does Mandy
Hope. Join her for all sorts of animal
adventures, at Animal Ark!

The Playful Puppy

Mandy thinks Timmy, Peter Foster's new puppy,
is adorable . . . but he chews things he shouldn't!
Can Mandy help to find Timmy a less naughty
game to play?

The Curious Kitten

Shamrock is a tabby kitten, with bright green
eyes and tiger stripes. When Shamrock goes
outside for the very first time, he soon runs
into trouble . . .

The Midnight Mouse

Mandy is helping Amy Fenton to choose just
the right mouse to be her pet. But they can't
think of the right name for her – until late at
night, when the girls hear a strange noise in
Mandy's room . . .

Do you love animals? So does Mandy Hope. Join her for all sorts of animal adventures, at Animal Ark!

The Brave Bunny

Laura Baker's pet rabbit, Nibbles, is scared of everything! But now he must be brave – he is very ill. Will Mandy's dad find out what is wrong with Nibbles?

The Clever Cat

Friday is Mandy's favourite day at school. But during playtime, someone prints patterns all over the Art paper. Class 3's Art lesson is nearly ruined. Who could the mystery artist be?

The Cheeky Chick

Mandy's friends are bringing their pets to the Easter Festival. It's going to be great fun – especially as Charlie will be there. Charlie is the cheekiest chick that Mandy's ever met!

Do you love animals? So does Mandy Hope. Join her for all sorts of animal adventures, at Animal Ark!

The Happy Hamster

Tufty's fur isn't smooth and shiny like his brothers' and sisters'. No one seems to want the friendly little hamster. But Mandy soon helps to find Tufty a very special home. Best of all, it's just in time for Class 3's Pet Show!

The Proud Piglet

It's so hot! Mandy and her friends cool off by playing under the lawn sprinkler. But Rosy the piglet keeps cool another way – she jumps into the duck pond! Can Mandy help make Rosy a muddy, splashy place all of her own?

The Fearless Fox

Mandy thinks Hector the fox cub is great. He's definitely one of the most unusual animals she's helped her mum and dad to look after. But Hector is so brave, he doesn't seem to know that some things can be dangerous!

Look out for more titles coming soon from Hodder Children's Books